TULLUS
AND THE MONSTERS OF THE DEEP

TULLUS · 1ST CENTURY A.D. CHRISTIAN

Chariot Books™
David C. Cook Publishing Co.

Published by Chariot Books,
an imprint of David C. Cook Publishing Co.
David C. Cook Publishing Co., Elgin, Illinois 60120
David C. Cook Publishing Co., Weston, Ontario
Nova Distribution, Ltd., Newton Abbot, England

TULLUS AND THE MONSTERS OF THE DEEP
©1993 by David C. Cook Publishing Co.

Cover illustration by David Dorman
Cover design by Stephen D. Smith
Interior design by Paul Mouw

First printing, 1993
Printed in the United States of America
97 96 95 94 93 5 4 3 2 1

Library of Congress Cataloging-in-Publication Data
CIP applied for

Tullus and the Monsters of the Deep

Tullus is on his way to help some Christians establish a church on the island of Sicily. His ship has just entered the dreaded Strait of Messina --which separates Sicily from Italy-- when a sudden storm strikes!

ON EITHER WING, POWERFUL HELMSMEN STRAIN AGAINST THE STEERING OARS, TRYING TO KEEP THE VESSEL IN THE NARROW CHANNEL. THE SUPERSTITIOUS CREW IS BEGINNING TO PANIC.

WE ARE DOOMED! CHARYBDIS WILL SWALLOW THE SHIP AND ALL ON BOARD!

IF WE ESCAPE THAT FATE, SCYLLA WILL SURELY DEVOUR US!

THIS VOYAGE HAS BEEN IN TROUBLE FROM THE START.

AYE, IT'S THAT ROMAN PASSENGER. HE DID NOT MAKE A SACRIFICE TO NEPTUNE BEFORE WE SET SAIL.

ACCORDING TO ANCIENT ROMAN MYTHOLOGY, SCYLLA WAS ONCE A VERY BEAUTIFUL MAIDEN. SHE ANGERED THE ENCHANTRESS, CIRCE, WHO TURNED HER INTO A SIX-HEADED MONSTER. THE TERRIBLE BEAST SEIZED SAILORS FROM THE SHIPS THAT PASSED NEAR HER CAVE AND DEVOURED THEM.

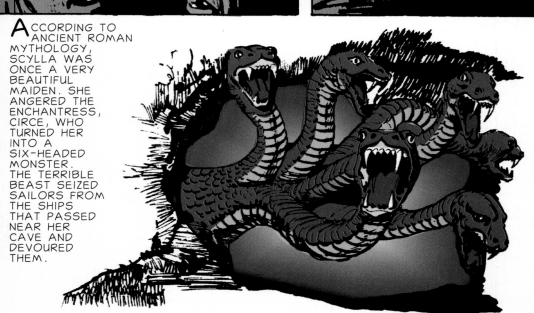

CHARYBDIS WAS SAID TO BE A MONSTROUS WHIRLPOOL. NO SHIP COULD ESCAPE ONCE IT WAS CAUGHT IN ITS SWIRLING GRIP!

TULLUS STANDS WITH THE CAPTAIN ON THE STERN OF THE HEAVING SHIP.

I DON'T WANT TO FRIGHTEN YOU, BUT WE WILL BE MORE THAN LUCKY TO GET THROUGH THIS NARROW STRAIT IN SUCH A STORM!

I HOPE YOU MADE A SACRIFICE TO THE GODS FOR A SAFE PASSAGE!

I NEVER SACRIFICE TO FALSE GODS.

NO SACRIFICES? THE GODS MAY BE FALSE AS YOU SAY, BUT I DON'T TAKE CHANCES. I PAY FOR SACRIFICES TO PLAY SAFE.

THESE SAILORS ARE VERY SUPERSTITIOUS. IT IS NOT WISE TO IGNORE THE GODS THEY BELIEVE IN.

I BELIEVE IN GOD. I AM A CHRISTIAN!

SUDDENLY THE SPOKESMAN THROWS HIS KNIFE AT TULLUS, BUT THE VESSEL LURCHES AND THE WEAPON STRIKES THE HELMSMAN! THE STEERING OAR SPINS WILDLY OUT OF HIS GRASP...

TULLUS GRABS THE BAR...

AND BRINGS THE SHIP AROUND, INCHES AWAY FROM THE SHARP TEETH OF A CRUEL ROCK.

BUT THIS DOES NOT QUIET THE SAILOR WHO STARTED THE MUTINY...

HE TURNED MY KNIFE AWAY BY WITCHCRAFT! HE WANTED THE HELMSMAN KILLED SO HE COULD STEER US INTO THE WHIRLPOOL! THROW HIM OVERBOARD!

7

JUST AS THE MEN START TO MOVE TOWARD TULLUS, THE SHIP'S BOW NOSES DOWN INTO A TOWERING WAVE SENDING TONS OF WATER ONTO THE DECK.

THE CAPTAIN TRIES TO BRING THE MEN BACK TO THEIR SENSES.

WITH NO EXPERIENCE, THIS YOUNG LAD HAS SAVED THE SHIP AND YOUR LIVES! NOW YOU, THERE! GET UP HERE AND RELIEVE HIM AT ONCE!

THE SAILOR OBEYS AND TULLUS GIVES FIRST AID TO THE WOUNDED MAN AND COVERS HIM WITH HIS ROBE.

MEANWHILE THE CAPTAIN HAS RESTORED SOME ORDER AMONG THE FRIGHTENED CREW. THE MAINSAIL IS LOWERED WHILE THE BOW SAIL IS SET TO HELP STEADY THE SHIP.

THE SHIP HAS REACHED THE NARROWEST PART OF THE DANGEROUS STRAIT. THE SAILORS HAVE ALMOST RECOVERED FROM THEIR PANIC. BUT THE BLACKNESS OF NIGHT IS NEAR.

SUDDENLY, OUT OF THE DARKNESS, A THORNBUSH BLOWN BY THE GALE LANDS AMONG THE CREW...

SCYLLA! THE MONSTER IS UPON US!

THE FEAR-RIDDEN CREW ADVANCES ON THE CAPTAIN AND TULLUS AS THE SHIP PLUNGES ALONG THROUGH THE DANGEROUS PASSAGE.

THE WOUNDED MAN PAINFULLY RAISES HIMSELF UP...

STOP! WHAT RIGHT HAVE YOU TO DEMAND THIS ROMAN'S LIFE?

YOU STRUCK ME WITH A KNIFE AND LEFT ME TO DIE. HE HELPED ME. I SAY **YOU** ARE THE MONSTERS!

AND YOU'RE COWARDS, TOO! YOU HAVE PUT ALL OUR LIVES IN DANGER BY LEAVING YOUR DUTIES TO CRY FOR THE BLOOD OF THIS INNOCENT ROMAN!

SUDDENLY THE BOW LOOKOUT WHO HAS STAYED AT HIS POST SCREAMS...

THE WHIRLPOOL! THE WHIRLPOOL! DEAD AHEAD!

THE FEAR-STRICKEN SAILORS RUSH TO THE ONE SMALL LIFEBOAT LASHED TO THE DECK. THE CAPTAIN, TRYING TO HALT THEM, IS THROWN TO THE DECK.

REALIZING ONLY DRASTIC ACTION WILL SNAP THE MEN OUT OF THEIR PANIC, TULLUS UNTIES A RUNNING LINE...

NOW COME TO YOUR SENSES! YOU SIX MEN GET ON THE OARS. YOU TWO GET READY WITH THE ANCHOR!

TULLUS'S FORCEFUL ACTION RESTORES THE SEAMEN TO THEIR USUAL OBEDIENCE.

TULLUS THEN TURNS TO THE CAPTAIN.

ARE YOU ALL RIGHT, CAPTAIN?

I--I THINK MY LEG IS BROKEN! YOU MUST TAKE CHARGE, TULLUS!

THE SMALL SHIP IS SWEPT INTO THE GRIP OF THE DREADED EDDY...WITHOUT A CAPTAIN!

THE SHIP AND CREW ARE IN YOUR HANDS. BRING US THROUGH SAFELY.

WITH GOD'S HELP I'LL DO MY BEST, CAPTAIN.

THE SHIP IS CAUGHT IN THE POWERFUL CURRENT OF THE DREADFUL WHIRLPOOL THAT THE SUPERSTITIOUS SAILORS THINK IS THE MYTHICAL MONSTER, CHARYBDIS.
THE GALE IS LETTING UP A BIT, SO TULLUS ORDERS THE SQUARE MAINSAIL HOISTED TO HELP THE SIX OARSMEN BREAK OUT OF THE EDDY. IT SEEMS HOPELESS! ROUND AND AROUND THE SHIP IS CARRIED BY THE SWIFT CURRENT. EACH TURN SWEEPS IT CLOSER TO THE GIANT ROCK...TO JOIN THE COUNTLESS OTHERS THAT HAVE LOST THE BATTLE WITH CHARYBDIS!

TULLUS SILENTLY PRAYS FOR GUIDANCE WHILE HE ENCOURAGES THE WEARY CREW.

WE'RE WINNING, MEN. SEE? THE WIND IS NOW HELPING US.

YOU TWO MEN, TAKE AN ANCHOR EACH. HEAVE IT AS FAR AS YOU CAN ON THE OUTER SIDE OF THE EDDY, THEN PULL IT IN AND REPEAT.

THIS ROMAN IS SMART!

AYE, WE'RE BEGINNING TO GET OUT OF THE CURRENT.

IT'S DAWN BEFORE THEY FINALLY GET THE SHIP TO A SAFE COVE AND BEACH IT. EVERYONE TAKES A MUCH-NEEDED REST.

TWO DAYS LATER THEY REACH THE CITY WHERE TULLUS IS GOING TO HELP ESTABLISH A CHRISTIAN CHURCH.

TULLUS HAS ASKED ME NOT TO BRING A CHARGE OF MUTINY AND ATTEMPTED MURDER AGAINST YOU.

YOU DID YOUR DUTY AS SOON AS YOU GOT OVER YOUR FEAR. YOU ARE ALL INVITED TO OUR NEW CHRISTIAN CHURCH ... TO GIVE THANKS FOR OUR SAFE ARRIVAL.

LET'S ALL GO!

Tullus

and the Horse of Dacia

TULLUS
AND THE HORSE OF DACIA

TULLUS HAS GONE TO DACIA (NOW ROMANIA) IN ASIA MINOR TO PURCHASE A HORSE FOR HIS FRIEND MARCUS, OWNER OF A LARGE HORSE FARM NEAR ROME.

MARCUS'S AGENT IN DACIA, NAMED SETH, HAS GUIDED TULLUS TO THE ANNUAL HORSE FAIR HELD BY THE WILD NOMADS OF THE NORTHERN PLAINS.

THERE IS THE ENCAMPMENT. I SEE THE STALLION BATTLES ARE ALREADY UNDER WAY!

YOU MEAN THEY TRAIN THEIR HORSES TO FIGHT?

THAT'S HOW THEY JUDGE THE COURAGE AND STAMINA OF A BREED--SO IMPORTANT ON THEIR STEPPES WHERE WOLF PACKS ARE A CONSTANT PROBLEM.

THEY DON'T KEEP THEIR HORSES WITHIN WALLS AT NIGHT?

17

A HUNDRED HOOVES THUNDER ACROSS THE PLAIN AS THE WILDLY YELLING NOMADS RACE TO CATCH TULLUS AND SETH!

THE REST OF THE PEOPLE AT THE CAMP LINE UP, FORMING A LINE TO THE POLE AS THEY WATCH.

18

BLAZE EASILY OUTRUNS THE NOMADS' HORSES. BUT SETH IS NOT SO FORTUNATE.

YOU'RE MY CAPTIVE!

HO! THEY CAUGHT SETH! BUT THEY'LL NEVER CATCH US. RIGHT, BLAZE?

WE'RE ALMOST TO THE POLE, BLAZE. WE'LL WIN FOR SURE!

SUDDENLY FROM OUT OF THE CROWD...

... YET TULLUS IS FIRST TO THE POLE!

AND THE FRANTIC MOTHER RUSHES TO CLAIM HER CHILD.

20

22

AS TULLUS AND SETH START OFF TO INSPECT SOME HORSES...

I DID NOT THANK YOU FOR SAVING MY SON'S LIFE. I WAS TOO UPSET. I CAN REPAY YOU ONLY WITH A WARNING...

THE MONGOL WHO CHALLENGED YOU IS BOASTING HE WILL GET YOUR HORSE NO MATTER WHAT THE OUTCOME OF THE BATTLE. DO NOT LEAVE YOUR MOUNT UNATTENDED DAY OR NIGHT!

LATER...

SEE THOSE TWO HORSEMEN, TULLUS? ONE IS A GREEK HORSE DEALER. BUYERS WATCH THESE BATTLES FOR JUDGING A HORSE'S PEDIGREE!

I SUPPOSE THAT'S BECAUSE THESE NOMADS NEVER KEEP WRITTEN RECORDS AND A SELLER WILL NATURALLY SAY HIS ANIMALS ARE BEST!

23

24

25

SUDDENLY A GROUP OF HORSEMEN GALLOPS BETWEEN THEM...

THE STAMPEDING HORSES SWERVE AWAY. THEN A LONE RIDER RACES UP...

THAT WAS AN ATTEMPT TO FRIGHTEN YOU OFF BEFORE YOUR HORSE BATTLES THE MONGOL'S. DON'T LET IT. WE NOMADS WILL SEE THAT THE BATTLE IS FAIR!

I CAN'T HELP FEELING THAT STAMPEDE LAST NIGHT WAS MORE IN FUN THAN ANYTHING.

YOU MAY BE RIGHT. THESE WILD MONGOLS LOVE CRAZY JOKES.

HO! THE BEST GLADIATOR IN ROME COULDN'T ASK FOR A BETTER CROWD!

AND BLAZE HAS NO IDEA WHAT IT'S ALL ABOUT!

TULLUS AND THE MONGOL LEAD THEIR HORSES INTO THE RING...

THE MONGOL'S TRAINED FIGHTING HORSE IMMEDIATELY LUNGES AT THE SURPRISED BLAZE WHO TURNS AWAY FROM THE SUDDEN ATTACK.

27

AS BLAZE TURNS AWAY, THE ONLOOKERS GROAN IN DISMAY--ALL EXCEPT THE MONGOLS, WHO YELL WITH DELIGHT!

BUT BLAZE TURNED ONLY TO DELIVER A VICIOUS KICK WHICH TAKES ALL THE FIGHT OUT OF HIS OPPONENT!

THE MONGOLS QUICKLY STRIKE THEIR TENTS AND GALLOP OFF WITH THEIR LIVESTOCK!

I THINK NEXT YEAR WE'LL FORBID THE STALLION FIGHTS.

BLAZE, YOU SURPRISED ME! WHERE'D YOU LEARN THAT TRICK?

BUT BLAZE MERELY SHAKES HIS HEAD AND GALLOPS OFF.

TULLUS, A YOUNG ROMAN IN BIBLE TIMES, HAS REACHED THE BORDER OF WHAT IS TODAY WESTERN PAKISTAN. AT A TURN IN THE ROAD HE IS CONFRONTED BY A SMALL BOY WIELDING A MAN-SIZED SCIMITAR.* BEHIND THE BOY IS A WRECKED CART AND A WEEPING WOMAN.

*A SABER, HAVING A CURVED BLADE, USED BY WARRIORS IN EASTERN COUNTRIES.

STOP WHERE YOU ARE! DISMOUNT AND HAND YOUR HORSE OVER TO ME!

YOU'RE IN TROUBLE. HOW CAN I HELP YOU?

I DON'T NEED YOUR HELP. GIVE ME THE HORSE OR YOU'LL FEEL THE BITE OF MY BLADE.

SO! YOU WOULD ROB ME! AREN'T YOU A BIT YOUNG TO BE A HIGHWAYMAN?

HIGHWAYMAN? I AM PRINCE BHARAT. I'LL TEACH YOU TO...

RUSHING FORWARD, THE BOY SWINGS AT TULLUS, BUT THE HEAVY SCIMITAR SPINS HIM OFF HIS FEET. THE WEAPON FLIES CLATTERING OFF INTO THE BUSHES.

THAT CAN HAPPEN TO THE MIGHTIEST OF WARRIORS, O PRINCE. LET ME HELP YOU UP, BUT PLEASE, NO MORE SWORDPLAY!

YOUR HIGHNESS! ARE YOU HURT?

I'M NOT HURT AND I WILL NOT BE LAUGHED AT! IF MY FOOT HADN'T SLIPPED, I'D HAVE SLAIN YOU AND TAKEN YOUR HORSE.

I'M SURE YOU WOULD HAVE, PRINCE. BUT WHAT ARE YOU TWO DOING ON THIS LONELY ROAD WITH A WRECKED CART?

OH, SIR, WHEN THE WHEEL BROKE, OUR DRIVER WENT OFF WITH THE BULLOCKS AND NEVER RETURNED!

WE'VE BEEN WAITING HERE WITHOUT FOOD OR WATER ALL DAY!

HMM-- THIS WHEEL IS BROKEN BEYOND REPAIR.

THIS STRANGER IS SNEERING AT ME!

YOUNG PRINCE BHARAT HAS SLIPPED AWAY UNNOTICED BY TULLUS AND THE WOMAN, WHO IS THE PRINCE'S NURSE. THE BOY FINDS HIS SCIMITAR IN THE BUSHES BESIDE THE ROAD. NOW, TRAILING THE HEAVY WEAPON BEHIND HIM, HE CREEPS UP ON TULLUS.

I'LL TEACH HIM TO SNEER AT ME--PRINCE BHARAT!

31

WHILE TULLUS IS SCOLDING THE YOUNG PRINCE, TWO MOUNTED MEN APPEAR, UNNOTICED...

THAT'S THE PRINCE. JUST WHERE WE WERE TOLD HE'D BE.

IGNORE THE MAN AND WOMAN--GRAB THE BOY--COME!

LIKE A WHIRLWIND THE TWO HORSEMEN CHARGE THEM, AND BEFORE ANYONE CAN MOVE, THEY GRAB THE PRINCE...

...SWING HIM UP BEFORE ONE OF THEM, AND GALLOP OFF, DISAPPEARING IN A CLOUD OF DUST!

AYEE! THEY HAVE STOLEN THE PRINCE! ALL IS LOST--ALL IS LOST!

AYEE, AYEE, ALL IS LOST! THEY HAVE THE PRINCE--IT WAS FORETOLD THIS WOULD HAPPEN. AH, WOE, WOE!

STOP WAILING AND MAKE SOME SENSE. WHO ARE THEY, AND WHAT WAS FORETOLD?

TULLUS TRIES TO CALM THE BOY'S HYSTERICAL NURSE SO THAT HE CAN UNDERSTAND HER WILD RAVING AND PLAN THE BOY'S RESCUE.

NOW LISTEN TO ME. IF THE BOY IS TO BE RESCUED, I MUST KNOW WHO THOSE MEN WERE AND WHY THEY TOOK THE PRINCE.

IT WAS FORETOLD BY A SOOTHSAYER THAT THE PRINCE WOULD BE TAKEN AND NEVER AGAIN WOULD HE PRAY BEFORE SIVA. THAT CAN ONLY MEAN HE WILL BE KILLED!

NEVER MIND THE SOOTHSAYER--DO YOU KNOW WHO WOULD WANT TO KIDNAP THE PRINCE AND WHY?

BY THEIR DRESS I KNOW THE MEN ARE WARRIORS OF A KING WHOSE KINGDOM BORDERS ON THE PRINCE'S REALM. OUR RAJAH,* THE PRINCE'S FATHER, AND THE OTHER KING HAVE BEEN ENEMIES FOR MANY YEARS.

NOW THE PRINCE IS IN THEIR POWER AND THE PROPHECY WILL COME TRUE. YOU CAN DO NOTHING--NO ONE CAN.

WITH GOD'S HELP, I WILL TRY.

* TITLE OF AN INDIAN KING

34

WHILE THEY RIDE TO THE NEAREST VILLAGE, THE NURSE TELLS TULLUS ABOUT THE CONSTANT WARRING BETWEEN THE TWO LITTLE KINGDOMS.

NO MATTER WHAT OUR RAJAH PAYS FOR PRINCE BHARAT'S RELEASE, THEY WILL NEVER LET HIM GO. HE IS LOST TO THIS LIFE!

WHY CAN'T HE BE RANSOMED?

YOU ARE A STRANGER IN THIS LAND. YOU DO NOT UNDERSTAND THE HATREDS THAT CAN DEVELOP UNDER OUR CASTE SYSTEM.

THOUSANDS OF YEARS AGO THE ARYANS INVADED INDIA AND CONQUERED THE ORIGINAL INHABITANTS, THE DRAVIDIANS.

TO SEPARATE THE PEOPLE, THE CONQUERORS ESTABLISHED A CASTE SYSTEM WHICH HAS CAUSED GREAT HATRED AMONG OUR PEOPLE.

THERE ARE FOUR CASTES. PRIESTS AND SCHOLARS ARE BRAHMANS; RULERS AND WARRIORS ARE KSHATRIYAS; ARTISANS AND MERCHANTS ARE VAISYAS; UNSKILLED WORKERS ARE SUDRAS...

ALL OTHERS ARE CALLED PARIAHS. THEY ARE OUTCASTS AND UNTOUCHABLES.

BUT WHAT HAS THIS TO DO WITH THE KIDNAPPING OF PRINCE BHARAT?

HE AND HIS FAMILY ARE BRAHMANS. THE ENEMY KING WAS BORN A SUDRA WHO, BY MURDER AND GUILE, MADE HIMSELF RULER.

AH, I SEE. AND HE IS JEALOUS OF THE OTHER'S HIGHER CASTE!

AYE. TWO HORSEMEN RODE PAST. ONE HAD A BOY RIDING WITH HIM.

THEY TOOK THE ROAD THAT LEADS INTO THE HILLS.

WHEN TULLUS AND THE NURSE, MARI, REACH A NEARBY VILLAGE...

IT IS AS I FEARED! THEY ARE TAKING HIM TO THE RAJAH'S ENEMY! NO ONE CAN SAVE HIM NOW!

DON'T GIVE UP HOPE. AT LEAST WE KNOW WHERE THEY ARE HEADING.

TULLUS STOPS IN THE VILLAGE ONLY LONG ENOUGH TO BUY FOOD FOR HIMSELF AND BLAZE. THEN HE CAREFULLY MEMORIZES THE DIRECTIONS TO THE KINGDOM WHERE THE KIDNAPPERS ARE CARRYING PRINCE BHARAT, AND STARTS OFF IN PURSUIT...

IT'S UP TO US, BLAZE. THEY HAVE A TWO-HOUR START ON US...

BUT I HAVE A FEELING THAT PRINCE BHARAT WILL SLOW THEM DOWN A BIT!

AND TULLUS IS RIGHT!

WHAT'S THE TROUBLE NOW? YOU'RE DELAYING US. CAN'T YOU HANDLE HIM?

IF YOU THINK YOU CAN HOLD THIS SQUIRMING SNAKE, TAKE HIM!

BUT SAYING IS EASIER THAN DOING!

COME BACK, YOU LITTLE IMP!

YOU LET HIM GO BEFORE I HAD HIM!

UNMINDFUL OF POSSIBLE BROKEN BONES, PRINCE BHARAT SLIDES DOWN THE STEEP CLIFF BESIDE THE ROAD...

AND BY THE TIME THE TWO MEN CAN CALM THEIR HORSES AND FOLLOW, HE HAS DISAPPEARED!

WE'VE GOT TO FIND HIM, OR THE KING WILL HAVE OUR HEADS!

WE CAN'T SEARCH AMONG THESE BOULDERS WITH THE HORSES!

HOBBLE THEM HERE. THAT LITTLE IMP CAN'T BE FAR OFF.

FOR HOURS THE TWO MEN SEARCH THE AREA.

WHAT ARE WE GOING TO DO? THE BOY HAS VANISHED!

WE DARE NOT RETURN TO THE KING WITHOUT HIM! BUT IT WILL SOON BE DARK!

COULD INDRA, THE GOD OF A THOUSAND EYES, HAVE SEEN HIM ESCAPE AND CARRIED HIM AWAY?

IT WOULD BE BETTER FOR US IF INDRA WOULD USE HIS EYES IN OUR BEHALF!

THEY'RE FAR OFF! NOW'S MY CHANCE TO GET AWAY!

KEEPING BEHIND THE BOULDERS, PRINCE BHARAT MAKES HIS WAY TOWARD THE HORSES...

AND QUICKLY REMOVES THEIR HOBBLES...

THEN, MOUNTING ONE AND LEADING THE OTHER, URGES THEM UP THE CLIFF!

THE HORSES! THEY'RE LOOSE!

HA! THE PRINCE THINKS HE CAN ESCAPE ON THEM! HE WON'T GET FAR!

GO, STEED, GO! EXTRA BARLEY AND OATS FOR THE REST OF YOUR DAYS IF I ESCAPE!

BUT ONE OF THE MEN PUTS HIS FINGERS TO HIS MOUTH AND WHISTLES SHRILLY...

AND THE WELL-TRAINED HORSES OBEY THE SIGNAL, REFUSING TO BUDGE DESPITE ALL THE BOY'S URGING.

GO! GO! MOVE YOU STUPID BEASTS, MOVE!

IN THE DARKNESS THE BOY CAN HEAR THE RATTLING OF STONES AS THE TWO MEN MAKE THEIR WAY UP THE CLIFF. FRANTICALLY HE KICKS AND URGES THE HORSES ON, BUT TO NO AVAIL. THE OBEDIENT HORSES STAND FAST WAITING FOR THEIR MASTERS.

WHEN WE GET OUR HANDS ON HIM, HE'LL NEVER TRY TO ESCAPE AGAIN!

AYE! BUT WE MUST KEEP HIM ALIVE UNTIL WE DELIVER HIM TO THE KING!

40

PRINCE OR NOT, WHEN WE GET OUR HANDS ON HIM, HE'LL WISH HE'D NEVER SEEN A ROCK!

SUDDENLY FROM DOWN THE ROAD, THE PRINCE HEARS THE BEAT OF GALLOPING HOOVES...

PRINCE BHARAT! WHAT'S GOING ON?

OH, IT'S YOU! I WAS JUST GOING TO KNOCK YOU OFF YOUR HORSE!

WITHOUT STOPPING HIS ROCK THROWING, THE BOY TELLS TULLUS WHAT HAS BEEN HAPPENING.

AND THAT'S IT. BUT DON'T JUST STAND THERE...THROW SOME ROCKS!

YOU CAN'T KEEP THROWING ROCKS ALL NIGHT! COME, WE CAN GET AWAY ON MY HORSE, BLAZE!

ALL RIGHT, BUT LET ME ROLL THIS BIG ROCK DOWN FIRST!

JUST AT THAT MOMENT THE MAN WHO HAD CLIMBED THE CLIFF FROM ANOTHER DIRECTION REACHES THE RIM OF THE ROAD...

NOW, I'LL RUSH HIM AND PUT AN END TO THIS NONSENSE!

BUT AS HE SCRAMBLES OVER THE RIM, THE EDGE CRUMBLES UNDER HIS WEIGHT AND HE ROLLS BACK DOWN THE HILL.

WHERE ARE YOU GOING!

SOMETHING FELL DOWN THE CLIFF...

COME BACK HERE. WE'VE GOT TO GET AWAY!

AW.

WHY DON'T WE TAKE THEIR HORSES?

BECAUSE THAT WOULD BE STEALING.

43

WE'RE FAR ENOUGH AWAY NOW TO GIVE BLAZE A BREATHER. WHOA, BLAZE, SLOW DOWN TO A WALK.

THOSE WERE EVIL MEN, YET YOU SAID IT WOULD BE STEALING TO TAKE THEIR HORSES. I DON'T UNDERSTAND.

TAKING ANYTHING THAT DOES NOT BELONG TO YOU IS STEALING. THOSE MEN ARE EVIL, BUT THAT'S NO EXCUSE FOR YOU TO DO WRONG.

I AM A PRINCE AND A BRAHMAN. NOTHING I DO CAN BE WRONG!

I AM A CHRISTIAN. I TRY TO DO NO WRONG.

AS THEY RIDE ALONG, TULLUS TRIES TO EXPLAIN WHAT IS RIGHT AND WRONG ACCORDING TO CHRIST'S TEACHINGS.

BUT THE LITTLE PRINCE'S HEAD DROOPS LOWER AND LOWER...

OH-OH, ASLEEP. NO WONDER. HE'S HAD QUITE A BUSY DAY!

PULLING OFF THE ROAD INTO THE HIGH GRASS WHERE THEY WILL BE WELL HIDDEN, TULLUS GENTLY LAYS THE SLEEPING BOY DOWN AND FALLS FAST ASLEEP HIMSELF.

IN THE MEANTIME, THE TWO WOULD-BE KIDNAPPERS HAVE REGAINED THEIR HORSES.

WHAT DO WE DO NOW? WE'VE SEARCHED ALL AROUND HERE, BUT THAT LITTLE IMP HAS COMPLETELY DISAPPEARED!

'TIS AS THOUGH SOME GENIE HAS FLOWN AWAY WITH HIM!

WE DARE NOT RETURN TO OUR KING WITHOUT THE PRINCE!

I VOW TO YOU NOW, I WILL RECAPTURE THAT BOY AND DRAG HIM TO THE KING TIED TO MY HORSE'S TAIL!

TO BE CONTINUED IN TULLUS AND THE KIDNAPPED PRINCE PART II

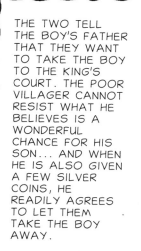

THE TWO TELL THE BOY'S FATHER THAT THEY WANT TO TAKE THE BOY TO THE KING'S COURT. THE POOR VILLAGER CANNOT RESIST WHAT HE BELIEVES IS A WONDERFUL CHANCE FOR HIS SON... AND WHEN HE IS ALSO GIVEN A FEW SILVER COINS, HE READILY AGREES TO LET THEM TAKE THE BOY AWAY.

Tullus and the
Dark City

Tullus and the
Death Race *

Tullus and the
Raging Bulls *

*coming soon